THE RAMESES' REVENGE

9th CINEBOOK
The 9th Art Publisher

Original title: Papyrus – La vengeance des Ramsès

Original edition: © Dupuis, 1984
by De Gieter
www.dupuis.com

English translation: © 2007 Cinebook Ltd

Translator: Luke Spear
Lettering and Text layout: Imadjinn sarl
Printed in Spain by Just Colour Graphic

This edition first published in Great Britain in 2007 by
CINEBOOK Ltd
56 Beech Avenue
Canterbury, Kent
CT4 7TA
www.cinebook.com

A CIP catalogue record for this book
is available from the British Library

ISBN 978-1-905460-35-9

9th CINEBOOK
The 9th Art Publisher

Huh?!... Where are we?

Papyrus! By Isis, you're still asleep! We're on the royal galley and we've been sailing for 4 days, heading for Abu-Simbel* and the great temple of Rameses II, with the whole of my father the Pharaoh's flotilla.

*Situated in Egyptian Nubia, where Rameses II had 2 temples built for himself and for his wife Nefertari.

WADI ES-SEBOUA IN SIGHT!

Wadi Es-Seboua! The last town before Abu-Simbel that Pharaoh has yet to honour with his presence! The garrison is already in the port!

And there, Princess, the priests and all the little people!

Have you seen, Papyrus?

Papyrus? He's gone!... Where'd he go? Papyrus!

Papyrus heard nothing. Bowled over by the vision from his dream, he crossed the galley.

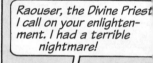

Raouser, the Divine Priest I call on your enlightenment. I had a terrible nightmare!

Is that you, Papyrus? Come in!

In a few words, Papyrus told of his dream.

...And I woke up in a daze!

Beware, Papyrus! By Divine Horus, you are in danger. Your vision is a warning. Alas, your brutal awakening prevents me from saying any more!

Go now! But beware!

Papyrus!

Come quick! I've got some good news for you!

All starboard!

Haul in the sail! Bring in the oars!

You've been complaining about how slow the voyage was since we left, and the royal flotilla will stay here for two more days to pay homage to the Gods in Rameses' temple!

I know, and so?

Well! No more boring receptions. We're not disembarking! I managed to convince the Pharaoh, my father. Tomorrow at dawn we'll head straight for Abu-Simbel with a light sail and a few men!

WHAT!

That...That's not possible! It's...It's too dangerous! It's...it's...

Meanwhile, Nut the Goddess of the Sky swallowed the sun. Day moved over for night, while Pharaoh and his great royal wife moved into the town, surrounded by the guard and followed by a cortege of priests and dignitaries.

By Horus! You told me a hundred times that you were bored! That the receptions made you sick and that you only came to see the two most famous temples in all of Egypt! And now that I have permission to finally please you, you don't want to go!

With only a small escort, one...one bad meeting and we're done for. And, it seems quite all right here anyway... We could wait two or three days!...

Oh, that's great!!

YOU can wait! I'm going tomorrow morning with Imhotep!

That's not possible! He has to drive the royal chariot during the ceremonies!

YOU'LL drive Pharaoh's chariot!

And Imhotep will come with me. Theti-Cheri, the Royal Princess, has given the order!

Eh?!

Night fell aboard the royal galley.

Another round, mate!

No, no. It's time for me to crawl back into my bunk!

Already?

Tomorrow I leave at dawn with a few soldiers to accompany the Princess to Abu-Simbel!

May the night be good to you, Neferka!

DE GIETER

Did you hear that?

So, are you playing?

Bah! Probably just a fisherman throwing out his waste, or a diving hippopotamus!

SPLASH

The next morning...

Everything is ready, Princess! We can leave!

Err!... How about I go and look for Papyrus, perhaps...

NO! And I forbid anyone from saying his name in front of me during the voyage!

Where is the fourth soldier I assigned? We can't row with three people!...

Err!... We don't know!

He's not here yet!

He fell suddenly ill in the night, noble Princess. I am here to replace him, if I may, ma'am!

!

DE GIÉTER.

Good, good! I can't wait to leave. To the oars, men, and onward!

Pushed by the skilful rowers, the little sailboat left Wadi at the break of dawn.

We have to unfurl the sail!

No! There's no point! There's no wind; it would slow us down!

Later, Ra the Sun God was already high in the sky, but there wasn't the slightest breeze to ripple the water's surface.

The heat began to scorch the Nile. Only the noise of the oars broke the silence.

They navigated by oar all through the day.

I'm tired and there's still not even the slightest breeze!

By Anubis! It's a bad omen!

We should perhaps deploy the sail!

But there's no wind!

Yes, yes, the wind's coming, I can feel it!

!

You want us to blow on it, Imhotep!

Hohoho!

A bit of air at last—I won't turn it down!

BOOM!

WAAAAH!
I'm dead! Crushed! Smashed! Flattened! Floored!

I'm doing fine, thanks!

Papyrus! What are you doing here!

Well, having a bit of a nap!

What a coincidence!

Coincidence? My eye! You're in league with each other. You dared to disobey a Royal Princess's orders!

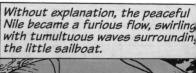

Summoned by the dazzling ray, an enormous beast emerged from a vast spray of water.

In a second, a panicked terror took hold of everyone.

WE'RE DONE FOR!!

AAAAH!!

Theti-Cheri stumbled and lost her balance.

LOOK OUT!

It's attacking the boat! Dive in! Quick!

Impossible! Theti is unconscious!

Then another beast surged from the foaming waters.

May the Goddess Isis help me to repel these monsters!

...With my pathetic weapon!

You forget, Papyrus, that your sword is magic and that it is always as brave as you are.

As brave as I? That's nothing. But it's all I have to fight them!

Barely touched by the magic blade, what had been a terrifying monster a moment before dissolved into a geyser that dropped back into the water.

Papyrus! Look out behind you!

That moment, the second creature was on him.

RRAAAAH RRAAAAH

This time, Papyrus gathered all of his courage and the blade was wondrous.

And, once again struck down, the monster transformed into a geyser.

The next moment, everything became peaceful once again.

Papyrus, what does all this mean?

Magic or nightmare, I don't know!

Ooooww! My head! What... what happened to me?

Theti-Cheri!

I took a big hit to the head, and after that I don't remember anything else!

By all the Gods, Princess! We were attacked by enormous beings! The Nile was furious! Ten times the boat nearly capsized! But Papyrus was here! He fought the monsters, risking his life! His blade became gigantic and he turned them into geysers and thus saved the boat!

Say now, Imhotep, I know your admiration for Papyrus. But don't you think that you're taking this one a bit too far?

Giant monsters? A furious river? All I see is a Nile that's perfectly still!

BOOM

Rocks! The current pushed us onto them!

R...ROCKS?! LOOK OUT!

DE GISTER

By Tawaret! These aren't rocks but hippos!

Let's get out of here before they get angry!

Indeed, driven mad by this intrusion on their territory, the colossal beasts burst into action with their mouths open, letting out terrifying cries.

GRROAAOO

An enormous male dove at Imhotep.

I...I can't swim! Help!

Emerging from the water with a snap, it threw the unfortunate fellow and crashed violently into another male...

GRROAWW

Imhotep!

Who turned to his attacker and engaged in a terrible fight.

Now's our chance. Quick! Let's try to reach the riverbank!

DE GIETER.

15

They're not following us!

So, Imhotep, what were you saying about Papyrus defeating monsters and saving boats!

Huh!

Nightfall found our three survivors trying to recover what they could.

The boat is really damaged!

And still no news about our escort soldiers. Perhaps they drowned!

Like I said from the start, this tr got off on the wrong foot. First t flat calm, then the storm and the monsters. These are all signs from the gods! We have to head back t Pharaoh as soon as we can!

Papyrus is right!

I don't believe one word of your stories. By Isis!

Ah! There they are, our escort soldiers. We'll ask them what happened!

We...We didn't see a thing, Princess!

The boat made a wrong turn that threw us overboard!

We tried to get back to you, but the boat was going too fast!

16

WHAT? You jumped into the water as soon as danger appeared and abandoned your princess, and now you pretend you didn't see a thing. B the gods! It's incredible! You deserve

Enough, Papyrus!

I make the decisions here. Don't forget that. We'll set up camp, and tomorrow I'll give counsel.

Night fell. After a frugal meal of honey cakes and fruits, they drifted off to sleep. The night watchman stood guard alone... well, nearly.

The next morning...

Princess, Princess!

What's wrong? What's happening?

Papyrus has disappeared and the guard has, too! We've been looking everywhere!

I'm not surprised. In his nervous state, he didn't manage to convince me against this trip, so he has gone back to Pharaoh. He won't have had any trouble convincing the guard!

But, Princess, Papyrus would never have abandoned you!

And yet that's what he's done!

But, Princess!

Enough! We'll leave immediately!

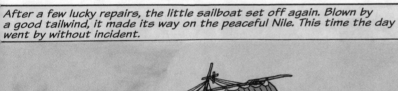

After a few lucky repairs, the little sailboat set off again. Blown by a good tailwind, it made its way on the peaceful Nile. This time the day went by without incident.

What do you think, Imhotep? Everything is going fine now that Papyrus isn't here! No more monsters or storms!

But Imhotep stayed silent. In front of him, the cliff suddenly seemed to open.

!

Then...

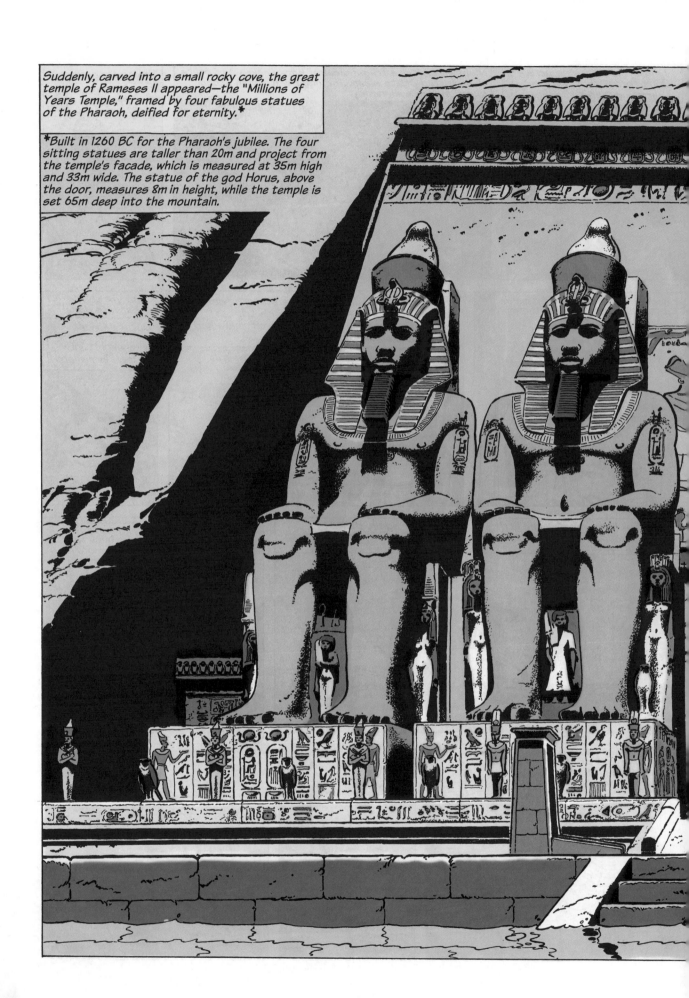

Suddenly, carved into a small rocky cove, the great temple of Rameses II appeared—the "Millions of Years Temple," framed by four fabulous statues of the Pharaoh, deified for eternity.*

*Built in 1260 BC for the Pharaoh's jubilee. The four sitting statues are taller than 20m and project from the temple's facade, which is measured at 35m high and 33m wide. The statue of the god Horus, above the door, measures 8m in height, while the temple is set 65m deep into the mountain.

Imhotep remained petrified by so much grandeur.

Hey, Imhotep, wake up and let the Princess by!

Wait there!

They had barely set foot on the esplanade when they were surrounded by armed men.

Halt!

Give yourself up! Resistance is futile!

Hey! Calm down, by Horus! Is this a way to receive an envoy from the Pharaoh?

The princess Theti-Cheri, heiress to the throne of the two Egypts!

For a moment the guard were stunned, but then...

Excuse us, Princess. We weren't told about your visit!

You were told about the Pharaoh's visit!

Err... yes...yes! Of course! When exactly will he be here?

Yet another two times will Nut swallow the sun god before the royal galleys will appear on the horizon.* I can't wait to visit the temple!

*According to legend, Nut, the sky goddess, swallowed the sun every night and brought it back to life every morning.

Of course! Of course! It's an enormous honour for your servant to be your guide, noble Princess!

HA! HA! HA!

!

Hahaha! Welcome to Abu-Simbel, beautiful Princess. It's a great honour for a pathetic priest like him to receive you. He can show you the treasures that he still refuses to share with me!

Who is this man? What does he mean?

Nothing, Princess, nothing! Come into the temple. The guards will silence this scoundrel!

Not so quick! Look who's under my control. Someone that you know quite well, Princess! Hahaha!

I don't believe it!

?

At the foot of the cliff, a group of bandits brutally led a young prisoner who was attached to a torturing plank, stumbling forward on the edge of total exhaustion.

Amongst his torturers, one of Pharaoh's soldiers.

By all the gods! PAPYRUS!

And there! The soldier who was the night watchman when they disappeared. It's the same man!

Yes, Papyrus is under my control. I've waited long enough. If half the temple's treasure isn't in my possession before the sun rises, he'll be put to death: Your only chance to save him is to convince this rogue, Princess! Hahaha!

27

No! Let Papyrus go! Don't hurt him. You can have anything you want!

Wretched dog! I'll get you one day!

...TOMORROW! BEFORE SUNRISE! HAHAHA!

The begging and pleading was to no avail as Papyrus disappeared, led away with a whipping.

We have to do something! We have to follow them!

Following them would be suicide. The garrison is too weak—we'd be decimated!

What then?

We can't do anything. Your friend is in the hands of the gods, Princess!

He's not in the hands of the gods but in the hands of those rogues who want half of this temple's treasure for his freedom! We have to give it to them!

The temple's treasure! That's unimaginable! Sacrilege! Nobody has the right to touch it! I can't accept that just for a mere fellah*!

As soon as Pharaoh arrives with his guard, he'll punish the looters and get back the treasure!

I give you my word!

No, no! It's impossible!

Enough! I want to see Hapu, the great priest of this temple!

He...he left to see Pharaoh. I'm in charge of the temple!

There isn't a wors[e] sacrilege than dis[obeying a represe[n]tative of the livin[g] god. By Pharaoh[,] I want to be obeye[d!]

* Fellah: A peasant, farmer or labourer. From the Arabic word for "ploughman"

Take me to the treasure chamber!

At your command, your Majesty.

After having passed through the entrance corridor, the small troop came into the immense hypostyle, supported by eight pillars and flanked by Rameses II's Osiris statues, which were wearing the white crown of high Egypt on the side and the double crown, the symbol of union between both Egypts, on the right.

Look out, here they come!

HALT! You are now entering the sanctuary. Only priests are allowed to enter!...

You too, of course, Princess. Your escort can rest and eat—this way!

23

A little later...

...mhotep briefly explained ...eir arrival at the temple!

But why did the priests take us prisoner?

You fell into a trap. The temple is in the hands of criminals. The garrison was attacked a few days ago. The guards were killed. Only Hapu, the high priest, managed to get away. We are the only survivors along with Userkere, the priest who welcomed you and who hopes to save his life by helping those scoundrels.

And the bandits who captured Papyrus?

A rival group, no doubt, who want half of the loot!

The funniest thing about it is that nobody knows where the treasure is hidden!

Only the high priest knows the secret. The bandits are searching for him in vain. The ...ope that one of us will give ...hem the clue has kept us ...live. But if they find him, ...e'll be finished. You people too, probably!

That means PAPYRUS IS LOST TOO!

...AND PRINCESS THETI-CHERI?

TRAITORS! THIEVES! YOU'VE GONE MAD! BY THE GODS, LET ME OUT!

BOOM BOOM BOOM

The Pharaoh's fury will follow you wherever you go!

Open this door!

BOOM BOOM

Let her whine! Did you hear that? The pharaoh will be here in two days. We have to find the treasure before then. Keep looking. Check the floor, the walls, the ceiling. Go! Get to work, by Anubis!

OK, OK! We're going!

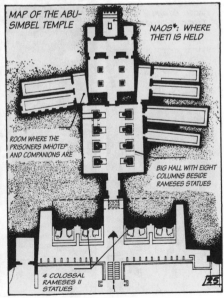

MAP OF THE ABU-SIMBEL TEMPLE

NAOS*: WHERE THETI IS HELD

ROOM WHERE THE PRISONERS IMHOTEP AND COMPANIONS ARE

BIG HALL WITH EIGHT COLUMNS BESIDE RAMESES STATUES

4 COLOSSAL RAMESES II STATUES

Naos: Every Egyptian temple has a naos, the most sacred room that houses a statue in the image of the god or goddess. The naos is also called "the holy of ...olies." In Greek and Roman temples (where it was called the cella), it also holds a statue of a god. The uninitiated could not enter into these rooms.

Did you hear that? She's going to let Pharaoh know about us and then he'll find us. If she recognises us, he'll be merciless. We have to finish her right now!

BOOM BOOM

Idiot! To kill a royal princess is the best way to put the whole Egyptian army on our heels. She will stay locked up in the naos. I know that there's nothing in there. We've searched it all, inch by inch!

If I give her back to Pharaoh in exchange for our freedom, he won't be able to refuse. But if we don't find this treasure fast you won't need pharaoh's mercy any longer.

Neither you, nor the other prisoners!

No, no! Don't kill me! Wait, I can help you!

Open the door! Don't go!

Have mercy!...

Oh, Papyrus! I wanted to save you. Alas! This time, the gods have abandoned us. All is lost!

And you, Ptah, Amon, Ramses and Ra, useless, stationary stone gods. You stand by watching the massacre of your servants and the pillaging of this temple. You all deserve to have your...

...NECKS WRUNG!

e end of the sentence sounded in the naos, aving Theti-Cheri stunned.

Am I dreaming?! I heard a voice that... that...

You aren't dreaming, Theti-Cheri! Twist the necks of each of the four gods!

This time, the order was given in an imperative tone. Theti-Cheri stood up like a robot.

Theti-Cheri stood dumbstruck for a moment at her audacity and at the result.

By the gods! About time, too!

DE GIETER

27

29

Hapu?! The temple's high priest! I thought you'd gone to meet Pharaoh!

Instead of asking questions, help me out of here. This secret passage isn't at all comfortable and I've been hidden in there for three days now!

Theti-Cheri! What a sight! What are you doing here? I was expecting Pharaoh, and here you are! Nevertheless, I sent you a magic message so that you'd turn back!

What... what do you mean?

By Ra-Horakhty! My powers won't let me leave without being seen. But I knew you were coming. By the solar disc, I sent a jet of fire to call the river spirits and to try to discourage you from your voyage!

?

That means Papyrus was right, and if he gets killed it'll all be my fault! I didn't want to listen to his advice!

Papyrus? Who's he?

I haven't got time to explain. My companion's life is in danger; he'll be burnt alive by the looters if they're not given the temple's treasures by sunrise. You have to help me and give them the gold. You know where it is!

Sweet, beautiful princess, calm down a little and explain it all!

Suddenly...

Watch out! I hear noises. Sounds like they're coming back!

Quick, this way!

I can't see anything!

And while the stone closed back in...

Carry on! Straight in front of you!

OH!

...fore her stunned eyes, a horde of golden objects: sceptres, ...s, vases, jewels, dishes, funeral masks, etc., all shining a dark ...endour in the weak light that penetrated the secret chamber.

By the gods! I've never seen anything like it!

...r a long while, Theti ...s quiet...

...ake this jewel—I give it ...o you by my high-priest ...owers!

No, no! I don't want anything for myself. Everything must go towards saving Papyrus. Pharaoh will compensate the temple. By Horus! I swear it! You have to help me, I beg of you!

But Princess, that's impossible! If we take the treasure from this hold, we'll inevitably fall into the hands of those who are occupying the temple!

Is there no other way than the naos?

...es! Through this corridor, ...e'll come out above the ...emple door, between the ...od Ra-Horakhty's feet!

Could I get out alone?

It's possible, but not worth it!

At nightfall, I'll go and hand myself over to the looters in exchange for Papyrus' life. I'll tell them where the treasure is. They wouldn't dare to hurt Pharaoh's daughter.

At these words, the high priest's face tightened.

No, wait!!

Those looters will **NEVER** own either the temple or you!

BY HORUS! THE GODS CANNOT ACCEPT SUCH AN INSULT!

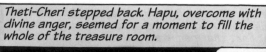

Theti-Cheri stepped back. Hapu, overcome with divine anger, seemed for a moment to fill the whole of the treasure room.

RA, LIVING SUN, GOD ABOVE GODS. Give me the power to burst forth your fury and to punish those wretches who have defiled your temple!

Walk, dog! We'll soon be done with you!

Tie him up here—the princess can watch his agony!

Suddenly...

BRR RR

DE GIETER

YOU, OH RA, LET YOUR POWER SHOW ITSELF THROUGH MY VOICE AND CRUSH THE DEFILERS OF YOUR NAME BY THE HAND OF THE FOUR RAMESES!

RAMESES! RAMESES! RAMESES! RAMESES!

Repeated four times, the name grew in volume and echoed between the vast walls of the two temples. Meanwhile, above the high priest, Ra's disc shone, equalling the brilliance of the sun.

Radiated by the shimmering rays, the giants seemed to tremble and then...

Moved by a supernatural force, the four stone giants stood, ripping their 1500 tonnes from the mountain.

The whole mountain shook. Guided by the magic of the disc, the fabulous giants began their INEXORABLE march.

Faced with this extraordinary, unheard-of phenomenon, the looters from both camps stood petrified with horror.

BOOM BOOOM

The...the giants! They're coming towards us!!

We're done for!

NOT YET! Let's hide in the small temple--it's our only hope!

Driven mad with fear, the bandits bolted into the queen's temple as quickly as they could.

Hurry up!

NO!

Without hesitating, the four Rameses plunged into the river.

But straightaway turned around and...

...shoulder to shoulder, formed a giant dam. In an instant, the mass of water carried by the river was stopped. The water foamed up, rose up the unbreakable giants...

Causing a giant wave, which submerged the barge and surged towards the temple in an instant.

The door, quick! Close the door!

PAPYRUS!

Leave him; he's in the hands of the gods!

For you, wretches, the time for your chastisement has come!

The water's rising! It'll drown us one by one!

Perhaps. By Anubis! But before that happens I'll silence this beast!

AAAGHH!

Hapu! High priest! By the gods! He's...

The high priest ceased to live. So, in an instant, the eye of Ra went out as the sky turned black, plunging the country into night.

The magical power that guided the giants was broken. They were suspended, disabled. But all of a sudden...

The elements went wild; the wind blew over the whole passage, picking up sand and speeding over the desert plateaus.

Let's close ourselves in the temple!

Staying outside would be risking certain death, yet...

...despite the sand that whipped her face, got in her eyes and nose, Theti-Cheri climbed down.

SLAM

Papyrus is in one of the giants' hands. I have to follow them!

By Isis! They're coming out of the water and heading for the mountain!

39

The storm blew harder, while the burning air became unbreathable.

I can't see any-more! I can't go any further...I...

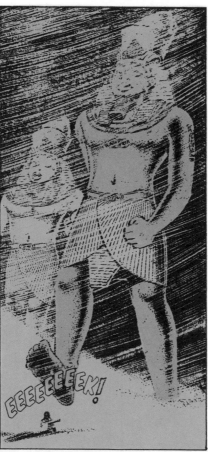

EEEEEEEEK!

Theti's cry of terror pierced the howling wind for a moment. Pulled out of his torpor, the giant hesitated...

He shook, tottered, incapable of holding up his enormous mass.

PAPYRUS

Suddenly...

BRAAOOOM

DE GIETER. 40

Papyrus! Are you ok?

Yes, I'm all right. The sand broke my fall!

We have to find shelter quickly!

It's too late!

Staying here is our only hope!

In the midst of the howling wind, the sandstorm carried on, implacable, remodelling the countryside.

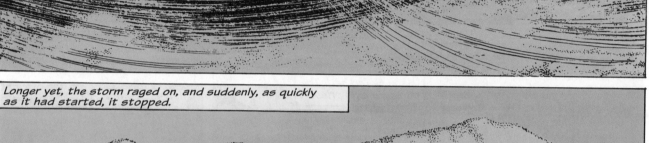

Longer yet, the storm raged on, and suddenly, as quickly as it had started, it stopped.

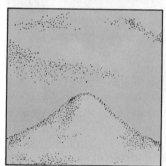

Theti-Cheri, are you all right? I think it's over!

!

OH! By the gods!

The giants have disappeared and the temples have been completely buried.

There are no more signs of life!

47

Yes! Look, Papyrus, over there! It's brilliant!

Hurrah! We're saved!

By Horus! Pharaoh's fleet!

A few moments later...

Theti-Cheri, my child, and you, Papyrus, you're safe and well!

Yes! We arrived just in time!

In the Pharaoh's shadow, a man spoke...

Hapu Neferkhet!! The temple's high priest?!

But...you were killed by a spear under the statue of Horus!

No, no! At the time of the looters' attack on the temple, I managed to get away and meet up with Pharaoh's fleet!

It's... it's not possible!

It really is possible, but forget about that. We have to give the order to dig out the temple as soon as possible!

Yes! The thieves and our escort are stuck inside!

You, too, you managed to escape!

Yes!...No!... I mean!...

Papyrus!

It's no use, nobody will believe us. Wait until they dig out the temple. When they see the statues missing, we'll explain it to them!

You're right!

With Pharaoh's camp set up, the soldiers worked in teams through the evening and into the night.

The following day...

Theti! Quick! Come see!

42

44

In no time, Theti-Cheri was outside and stopped, dumbfounded. Three quarters dug out, the giants appeared in their unmoving pose, seated on their thrones of rock... except for one.

What do you make of that?

Papyrus, I'm dreaming! The statues—we saw them disappear in the storm!

Look, lord Pharaoh. By the divine Horus! The violence of the elements has been so bad that one of the statues got broken!

No! It wasn't the storm that...

Theti, leave it!

Why try to explain the inexplicable. Only the gods know the truth!

I want to know it too. Come on!

Look out, the door is coming loose. Forward march!

No, no! We surrender!

Come on, bunch of rogues! Keep walking and no monkey business!

Papyrus!

Imhotep!

43

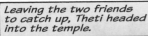
Leaving the two friends to catch up, Theti headed into the temple.

It's good to see you again!

I'll get to the bottom of this!

But this time, she tried in vain to make the heads turn.

Nnnng... Won't budge!

The death of the high priest, the temple treasure, walking giants, nothing existed. No, no, that's not possible.

THETI THETI THETI

Come quick!

Come see this!

Look there, in the broken statue's hand!

Looks like... it is! It's your sword!!

Indeed, it's my magic sword. The gods are giving it back to me!

So we weren't dreaming!

Seems not! Your golden necklace is another proof!

And the temple treasure exists!

No doubt. But it's a secret of the gods. Only a god could give you this gift!

He definitely took the form of the high priest to use you and to carry out Rameses' revenge!

You're right. I'll explain it all to them!

The high priest, a god?

No, no! Don't bother. Nobody will believe you. And don't forget that you are a little bit responsible for the damage at the temple... it's better that it stays between us!...

...and that this little story stops here. By Horus! I agree!

44

THE END

COMING SOON

APRIL 2008

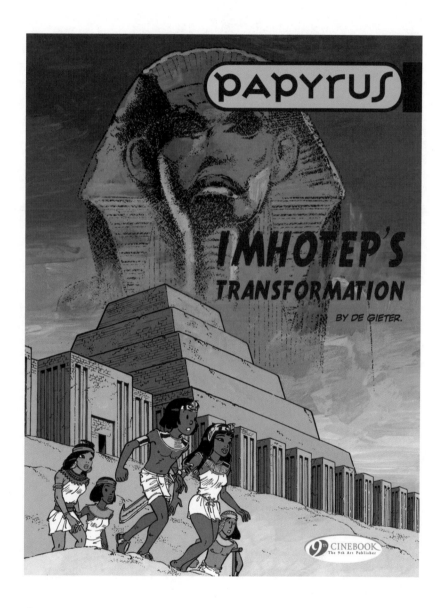

www.cinebook.com